KING COBRAS

by Jaclyn Jaycox

MW01078323

PEBBLE
a capstone imprint

Published by Pebble, an imprint of Capstone
1710 Roe Crest Drive, North Mankato, Minnesota 56003
capstonepub.com

Copyright © 2023 by Capstone. All rights reserved. No part of this publication may be reproduced in whole or in part, or stored in a retrieval system, or transmitted in any form or by any means, electronic, mechanical, photocopying, recording, or otherwise, without written permission of the publisher.

Library of Congress Cataloging-in-Publication Data
Names: Jaycox, Jaclyn, 1983- author.
Title: King cobras / by Jaclyn Jaycox.
Description: North Mankato, Minnesota : Pebble, [2023] | Series: Animals | Includes bibliographical references and index. | Audience: Ages 5-8 | Audience: Grades K-1 | Summary: "What is the longest venomous snake in the world? The king cobra! It can grow longer than a limousine. Its deadly bite can even take down an elephant. With easy-to-read facts and colorful photos, young readers will enjoy learning more about these fascinating reptiles"— Provided by publisher.
Identifiers: LCCN 2022000661 (print) | LCCN 2022000662 (ebook) | ISBN 9781666342765 (hardcover) | ISBN 9781666342802 (paperback) | ISBN 9781666342840 (pdf) | ISBN 9781666342925 (kindle edition)
Subjects: LCSH: King cobra—Juvenile literature.
Classification: LCC QL666.O64 J385 2023 (print) | LCC QL666.O64 (ebook) | DDC 597.96/42—dc23/eng/20220202
LC record available at https://lccn.loc.gov/2022000661
LC ebook record available at https://lccn.loc.gov/2022000662

Image Credits
Alamy: Malcolm Schuyl, 22; Capstone Press, 6; Getty Images: Cavan Images, 5, ePhotocorp, 11, Neeraj Sharma, 1, 8, R. Andrew Odum, 25, somdul, 18, Zocha_K, 12; Shutterstock: Aleksandar Kamasi, Cover, awo|666, 9, ccarbill, 21, DSlight_photography, 14, FERI ISTANTO, 26, Mufti Adi Utomo, 17, 28, Ondrej Prosicky, 7, Rich Carey, 27, vanGeo, 13

Editorial Credits
Editor: Abby Huff; Designer: Dina Her; Media Researchers: Jo Miller and Pam Mitsakos; Production Specialist: Tori Abraham

All internet sites appearing in back matter were available and accurate when this book was sent to press.

Table of Contents

Words in **bold** are in the glossary.

Amazing King Cobras

What snake mostly eats other snakes? A king cobra! It has a deadly bite. It's called "king" because it kills and eats other cobras.

King cobras are **reptiles**. They are cold-blooded. They can't control their body heat. When it's hot outside, they are hot. When it's cold, they are cold.

Where in the World

King cobras live in South and Southeast Asia. They are found in northern India and parts of China. They also live in Indonesia and the Philippines.

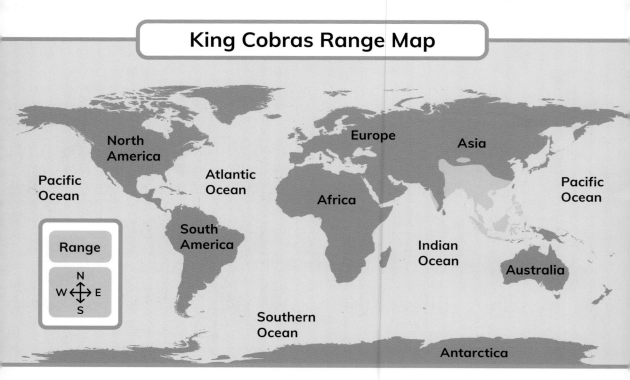

King Cobras Range Map

North America

Europe

Asia

Pacific Ocean

Atlantic Ocean

Pacific Ocean

Africa

South America

Range

N
W ⟷ E
S

Indian Ocean

Australia

Southern Ocean

Antarctica

Many king cobras live in hot, **tropical** areas. They can be found in rain forests. They live in grasslands and swamps too. King cobras often stay near water. Temperatures there remain mostly the same. It helps the snakes not get too hot or cold.

King cobras spend most of their
time on land. But they can swim too.
They are also great climbers. They
sometimes hang out in trees or bushes.

These animals don't make homes. Instead, they find shelter on the ground. They hide under logs. They slither into animal **burrows**. They squeeze into cracks in rocks.

King Cobra Bodies

King cobras are the longest **venomous** snakes in the world. They never stop growing. They can reach lengths of 18 feet (5.5 meters). That's longer than some pickup trucks!

King cobras have smooth scales. They can be black or brown. They can be yellow or green too. Their throats are often a lighter color. King cobras may have yellow or white stripes.

What makes a king cobra so deadly? Its bite! It has two **fangs**. When a cobra bites, **venom** flows out of the fangs. It goes into the **prey**. The venom is strong. It can kill a person in less than 30 minutes. It can even kill an elephant!

fangs

King cobras have great eyesight. They can see movement 330 feet (100 m) away. A cobra's tongue also helps with finding food. The tongue flicks out. It picks up scents from prey.

hood

When a king cobra feels it's in danger, it does things to make itself look bigger. This helps scare away **predators**.

The cobra lifts the front of its body off the ground. The skin on the sides of its neck flares out. This is the hood. Muscles and bones stretch out the skin.

On the Menu

A hungry king cobra slithers through the grass. It spots a snake. In a flash, the cobra bites. Its prey can't move. Time to eat!

King cobras hunt mostly during the day. They mainly eat snakes. They eat rat snakes and pythons. They eat other cobras. Some prey can be up to 10 feet (3 m) long. That's a big meal!

A king cobra at a zoo eats a frog whole.

King cobras don't use their fangs for chewing. Instead, they swallow prey whole. Their jaws open wide. A cobra can swallow prey bigger than its head! It's a slow process. It can take an hour to swallow large prey.

A cobra's body breaks down food very slowly. After a large meal, cobras can go many months before eating again.

Life of a King Cobra

Hiss! Grrr! King cobras use sounds to **communicate**. They are shy snakes. They usually try to escape danger. If they can't, they hiss as a warning. They even growl like a dog! It tells others to stay away. If that doesn't work, the cobra will attack.

King cobras live alone. They only come together to **mate**. A group of king cobras is called a quiver.

A hissing king cobra

King cobra eggs lay in a nest of leaves.

Female king cobras build nests. No other snakes do this. A female will push leaves with her tail to make a pile.

The female lays up to 40 eggs in her nest. She covers them in more leaves. It keeps the eggs warm. The female sits on the nest. The male stays close by. The two keep the eggs safe from predators. After two to three months, the eggs hatch.

Baby cobras are called hatchlings. They have black scales. They have yellow or white stripes too.

Parents don't take care of their young. They leave right before the eggs hatch. But babies are ready for life on their own. They are born with venom. They can hunt for food right away.

King cobras are adults after about five years. They can mate and lay eggs. These snakes can live about 20 years.

A baby king cobra breaks out of its egg.

Dangers to King Cobras

King cobras don't have many predators. Their venom helps keep them safe. But one animal is not hurt by venom. It's a mongoose. Some kinds eat snakes. They don't often hunt for king cobras. But a mongoose will attack if it comes across one.

mongoose

Forests where king cobras live are being cut down.

Humans are the biggest danger to king cobras. Some people hunt them for their skin. Others kill them out of fear. Humans are also cutting down rain forests. King cobras are losing their homes.

The number of king cobras is going down. But people are working to help. Laws in many areas keep people from hunting cobras. Groups teach others about the snakes so people aren't afraid. They want to keep these amazing animals safe.

Fast Facts

Name: king cobra

Habitat: rain forests, grasslands, swamps

Where in the World: South and Southeast Asia

Food: snakes

Predators: mongooses, humans

Life Span: 20 years

Glossary

burrow (BUHR-oh)—a hole or tunnel in the ground made or used by an animal

communicate (kuh-MYOO-nuh-kayt)—to pass along information, thoughts, or feelings to others

fang (FANG)—a long, hollow tooth; venom flows through fangs

mate (MEYT)—to join with another to produce young

predator (PRED-uh-tur)—an animal that hunts other animals for food

prey (PRAY)—an animal hunted by another animal for food

reptile (REP-tahyl)—a cold-blooded animal that breathes air and has a backbone; most reptiles have scales

tropical (TROP-ih-kuhl)—hot and wet; places near the equator are tropical

venom (VEN-uhm)—a poison made by some animals

venomous (VEN-uhm-us)—able to make a venom

Read More

Boutland, Craig. *King Cobra*. Minneapolis: Bearport Publishing Company, 2021.

Humphrey, Natalie. *King Cobra: Snake Eater*. New York: Enslow Publishing, 2021.

Murray, Julie. *King Cobras*. Minneapolis: Big Buddy Books, 2020.

Internet Sites

Critter Squad Wildlife Defenders: King Cobra Fact Sheet
crittersquad.com/fact-sheets/king-cobra-fact-sheet/

DK FindOut!: Cobras
dkfindout.com/us/animals-and-nature/reptiles/cobras/

National Geographic Kids: King Cobra
kids.nationalgeographic.com/animals/reptiles/facts/king-cobra

Index

About the Author

Jaclyn Jaycox is a children's book author and editor. She lives in southern Minnesota with her husband, two kids, and a spunky goldendoodle.